D0577173

JAKE GANDER

Storyville Detective

BY

GEORGE McCLEMENTS

HYPERION BOOKS FOR CHILDREN
New York

WITHDRAWN

UNIVERSITY OF NV LAS VEGAS
CURRICULUM MATERIALS LIBRARY
101 EDUCATION BLDG
LAS VEGAS, NV 89154

Text and illustrations copyright © 2002 by George McClements
All rights reserved. No part of this book may be reproduced or
transmitted in any form or by any means, electronic or mechanical, including
photocopying, recording, or by any information storage and retrieval system,
without written permission from the publisher. For information address
Hyperion Books for Children, 114 Fifth Avenue, New York, New York 10011-5690.

First Edition
1 3 5 7 9 10 8 6 4 2

Library of Congress Cataloging-in-Publication Data
McClements, George.
Jake Gander, Storyville detective / by George McClements.—1st ed.
p. cm.
Summary: A series of fairly obvious clues helps Jake Gander
prove Red R. Hood's suspicions about her granny's strange new look.
ISBN 0-7868-0662-1 (trade hc)
[1. Characters in literature—Fiction. 2. Mystery and detective stories.] I. Title.
PZ7.M1325 Jak 2002
[E]—dc21
2001016635

Printed in Hong Kong
Visit www.hyperionchildrensbooks.com

My name is Jake Gander.
I'm a cop. My beat: Storyville,
a fairy-tale town where
endings aren't always happy.

My job is to rewrite them.

Once upon a time . . .

I had just sat down to read
the paper when the phone rang,
shattering my quiet morning.

It was a **code P.W.T.** (Possible Wolf Trouble). I wrote down the address and hit the streets.

I pulled up to a house,
where I found one Red R. Hood.

I flashed my badge, and
she told me her story.

Red said that her granny had
a strange new look. Fur pajamas
that never came off, really
sharp teeth, and rabbit breath.

Hmmm . . .

I asked Red to take me to Granny.

When I walked in, I instantly knew something was wrong.

I couldn't put my finger on it, so
I decided to take our little party
downtown to clear things up.

At the station, I told Granny to cool her heels in the hot seat and began my investigation.

I looked at her ears.
They were large enough to butter.

I searched my files for a
standard-issue Ear Size
Comparison chart.

Just as I thought,
Granny's ears should
be as small as my
paycheck.

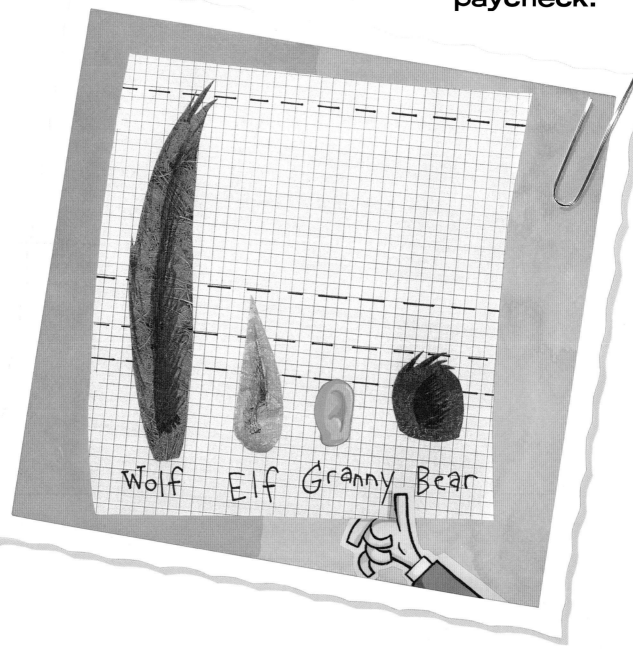

Wolf   Elf   Granny   Bear

My first clue.

Next, I checked the manhole covers she called eyes.

They seemed quite big.

I went to the storage room
to look for granny glasses.
All grannies in Storyville wore
standard #12 wire-frame bifocals.

With some quick calculations,
I discovered that something
was not adding up.

I was closing
in on an answer.

I moved on to Granny's
impressive set of choppers.

They were as sharp as
an aged piece of cheddar.

Fortunately, I had Granny's dental chart on file. She had a mouth like a river, but no sharp teeth.

I was so close to cracking
the case, I could taste it.
That's when Red stepped in.

She handed me THE BIG BOOK
OF FURRY THINGS, opened to W.
It took me only a moment to
find the final clue I needed.

It all came together now—the big ears, the large eyes, the gigantic teeth, the fur that shed nonstop.

Our phony Granny was none other than . . . Harry A. Wolf! (a.k.a. Big Bad).

I arrested Harry on one count
of impersonating a granny and
on four counts of shedding.

In an ironic twist of fate, he
is now working in the Hood
division of the Storyville Prison.

The case seemed to have wrapped up nicely, but one thing still troubled me. . . .

Where was Granny?

A postcard answered my question.

Our happy ending was cut
short by the arrival of
some unexpected visitors.
It was going to be a busy day.